For Fred J.

First published in Belgium and Holland by Clavis Uitgeverij, Hasselt – Amsterdam, 2010
Copyright © 2010, Clavis Uitgeverij

English translation from the Dutch by Clavis Publishing Inc. New York
Copyright © 2011 for the English language edition: Clavis Publishing Inc. New York

Visit us on the web at www.clavisbooks.com – www.guidovangenechten.be

Little Snowman Stan written and illustrated by Guido van Genechten
Original title: *Stanneke sneeuwmanneke*
Translated from the Dutch by Clavis Publishing
English language edition edited by Emma D. Dryden, drydenbks llc

ISBN 978-1-60537-108-5

This book was printed in June 2011 at erasmus-euroset n.v., Biezeweg 12, B-9230 Wetteren, Belgium.

First Edition
10 9 8 7 6 5 4 3 2 1

GUIDO VAN GENECHTEN

Little Snowman
Stan

Clavis

NEW YORK

AT THE VERY BEGINNING of the winter
someone built him from snow: Two little coals for eyes,
a carrot for a nose, a long scarf around his neck,
a floppy hat on his head, a fork in his hand, and
Little Snowman Stan was born.

And there Little Snowman Stan stood for days,
for weeks, for a very, very long time....

Even though every snowflake in his body was trembling to move, Little Snowman Stan stayed perfectly still. It was what snowmen did. Sadly, he looked towards one of the larger snowmen in front of him—he was still and unmoving as always. Little Snowman Stan thought he looked like a snow soldier with that silly bucket on his head.

If Little Snowman Stan even moved only an inch
every now and then (He couldn't help it that he had an itch
or that a dog might want to play with him, could he?),
Snow Soldier would shout at him: "Stop it! Stand still!"

And then Mister Tophat, the other large snowman
standing next to them, would add in a more kindly way,
"No, no, little one, don't move."

Days passed. Weeks passed. The snowmen continued to stand still. One morning a bird landed on Little Snowman Stan's carrot nose. "What is it like to move freely, friendly bird?" asked Little Snowman Stan. "Hush!" Mister Tophat whispered. "Silence!" Snow Soldier roared. Startled, the bird fluttered her wings. "You should try it for yourself, little snowman. You can be free, too …" Her words were lost in the wind as she flew off.

Was it true? Could Little Snowman Stan
really move freely as the bird had said?
But, no, a snowman can't move.
A snowman has to stand still. And silent.

"But, why?" Little Snowman Stan whispered late one night. "Why aren't snowmen supposed to move?" "Hush," Mister Tophat said. "Be still, Little Stan."
"No," Little Snowman Stan insisted. "I want to move!"
"Don't you dare!" Snow Soldier's warning rumbled like thunder.
"All snowmen stand still. That's the way it is and that is never going to change!"
"Don't worry. You'll get used to it, little one," Mister Tophat comforted.

"But I don't *want* to get used to it!"
Little Snowman Stan cried. "I want to move! I am going to move!"

"Forget it!" Snow Soldier commanded.

"Just you wait," Little Snowman Stan said,
and he threw his fork onto the snow.

"No! Don't do it, Little Stan!" Mister Tophat groaned.

"At ease!" Snow Soldier screamed. "Halt! This cannot be.
If you move, you will melt!"

But Little Snowman Stan was moving now
and he could not stop. Little Snowman Stan
ran and leapt and danced and jumped.
Little Snowman Stan slid and fell
and slid and fell some more....

Little Snowman Stan laughed in the moonlight
and threw snowballs all the way to the moon.
No, higher than the moon!

Little Snowman Stan found an abandoned bicycle in the snow. He hopped on and began to ride—he rode far away, over mountains and through valleys. Little Snowman Stan felt as though he could ride all around the world! He never looked up or back.

Little Snowman Stan rode until he reached a beautiful white plain. There, he saw a row of dancing, laughing snowmen.

"Hey, don't you all have to stand still?" Little Snowman Stan asked them.

"No, of course not!" the snowmen answered with glee. "Not here in Freezeland. Here in our home snowmen can move around as much as we like."

"But, aren't you afraid you will melt?"

The friendly snowmen sent Little Snowman Stan to talk with Alfred, the oldest snowman in Freezeland.

Alfred had lived a very long time and was very wise.
He had seen many parts of the big, wide world.

"Listen, Little Stan," Alfred said, "Almost all snowmen stand still.
They are frozen because they have never ever moved. Or they don't move
because they are afraid and prefer to stay in one familiar spot. Some of them
even believe that you'll melt from a little bit of movement!"

"Yes!" Little Snowman Stan nodded eagerly. "That's what the other
snowmen kept telling me!"

Alfred patted Little Snowman Stan's head. "That is nonsense.
Only the sun can make a snowman melt. And here in Freezeland, it is too cold
for the sun to shine. So the snowmen who live here never melt. You see?"

Little Snowman Stan nodded thoughtfully.
Tomorrow morning he would go back home to Mister Tophat,
Snow Soldier, and the others. He would tell them all about Freezeland....